RABBIT'S NEW RUG

To librarians, parents, and teachers:

Rabbit's New Rug is a Parents Magazine READ ALOUD Original — one title in a series of colorfully illustrated and fun-to-read stories that young readers will be sure to come back to time and time again.

Now, in this special school and library edition of *Rabbit's New Rug,* adults have an even greater opportunity to increase children's responsiveness to reading and learning — and to have fun every step of the way.

When you finish this story, check the special section at the back of the book. There you will find games, projects, things to talk about, and other educational activities designed to make reading enjoyable by giving children and adults a chance to play together, work together, and talk over the story they have just read.

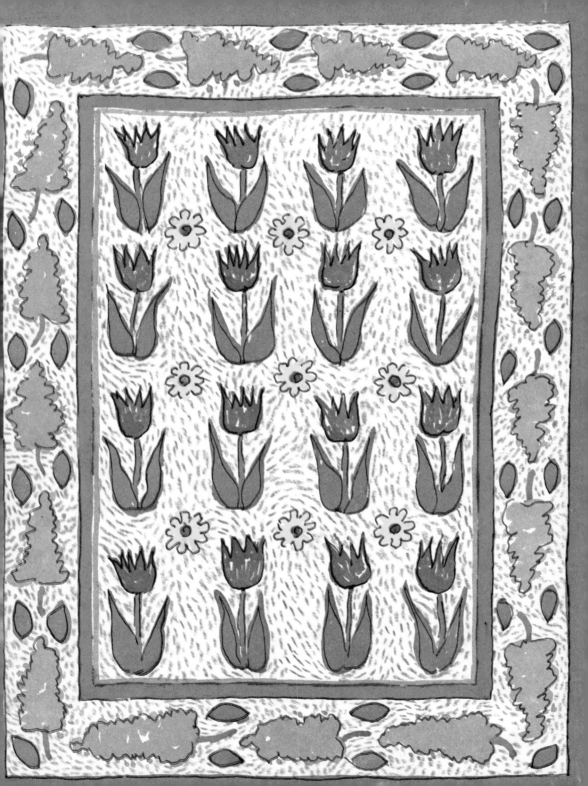

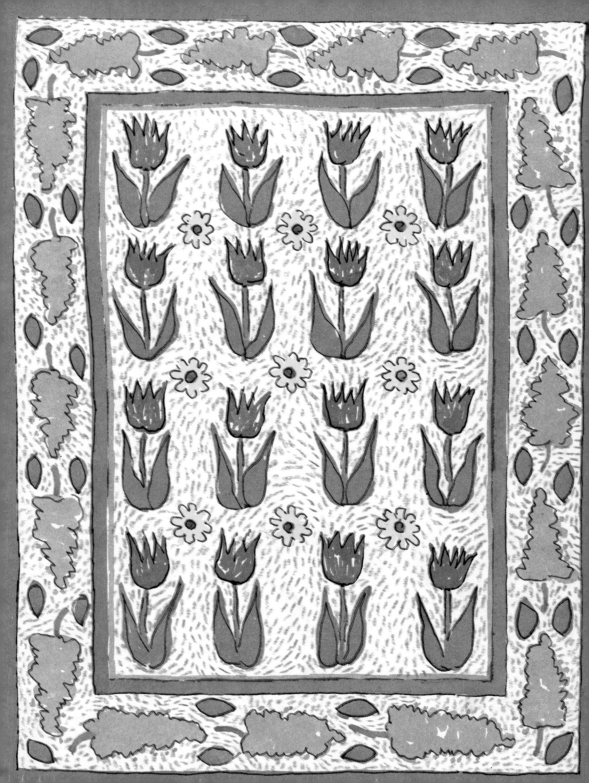

Library of Congress Cataloging-in-Publication Data

Delton, Judy.
    Rabbit's new rug / by Judy Delton; pictures by Marc Brown. — North American library ed.
      p. cm. — (Parents magazine read aloud original)
    Summary: Rabbit loves his beautiful new rug, but comes to realize there are more
important things.
ISBN 0-8368-0972-6
    [1. Friendship—Fiction. 2. Rabbits—Fiction.] I. Brown, Marc Tolon, ill. II. Title. III. Series.
  [PZ7.D388Rac 1993]
  [E]—dc20   93-15453

This North American library edition published in 1993 by Gareth Stevens Publishing,
1555 North RiverCenter Drive, Suite 201, Milwaukee, Wisconsin 53212, USA, under
an arrangement with Parents Magazine Press, New York.

Text © 1979 by Judy Delton. Illustrations © 1979 by Marc Brown. Portions of end
matter adapted from material first published in the newsletter *From Parents to
Parents* by the Parents Magazine Read Aloud Book Club, © 1989 by Gruner + Jahr,
USA, Publishing; other portions © 1993 by Gareth Stevens, Inc.

Printed in the United States of America

1 2 3 4 5 6 7 8 9 98 97 96 95 94 93

JUDY DELTON

RABBIT'S NEW RUG

PICTURES BY MARC BROWN

PARENTS MAGAZINE PRESS · NEW YORK

GARETH STEVENS PUBLISHING · MILWAUKEE

Rabbit had a new rug in his house.
The Flora Floor Store had just
delivered it.
The rug had large red tulips on it,
and small yellow daisies.
It had green leaves and
light blue snapdragons.

Rabbit clapped his paws together.
"My new rug is so pretty,
I'll call my friends over to see it."

10

Rabbit dialed Fox's number.

"I'll be over as soon as my strawberry jam is cooked," he said.

Then rabbit called Owl.

"I'll come as soon as I finish my nap,"
he said sleepily, looking at his watch.

Rabbit was waiting at his door
for his friends.

When Fox arrived, he looked over
Rabbit's shoulder at the new rug.
"What a beautiful rug!" he said.
"What fine-looking red flowers.
Red is my favorite color, you know."
Fox began to walk into the house.

14

"Don't walk on the rug!"
shouted Rabbit, holding up a paw.

"Look, Rabbit, you invited me over.
Am I supposed to stand outside?"

15

"Walk along the edges of the room, then,"
said Rabbit. "Just don't step on the rug."
Fox sighed and squeezed close to the wall.
"I hope you wiped your feet on the mat,"
scolded Rabbit. "You really should have
worn your galoshes in this weather."

"Rabbit! It is summer! No one wears
galoshes in summer! Here, I brought
a jar of jam for you."

"Thank you, Fox. But we'd better not open it. Some might get on my rug, and leave a terrible, sticky spot."

"It wouldn't show if it fell on the red flowers," said Fox under his breath.

Soon Owl came to the door.
He handed Rabbit a plate of brownies.
"From the bakery," he yawned.
"I wanted to bring a treat and I didn't
have time to bake so early in the day."

"Early!" said Fox. "It is two o'clock —
the day is half over."

"Not for me," said Owl.
"It hasn't even begun yet."

"Thank you for the brownies, Owl,"
said Rabbit.
"But we had better not eat them.
Someone might spill crumbs
on my new rug."

19

Owl looked at the rug.
"That is a fine rug, Rabbit.
Almost too pretty to walk on."

"That's why I'm standing here
near the wall," muttered Fox.

Just then Raccoon came by,
and looked in the door.
"Why, Rabbit! You have a new rug!"
he said. Then he noticed his
friends leaning up against the wall.

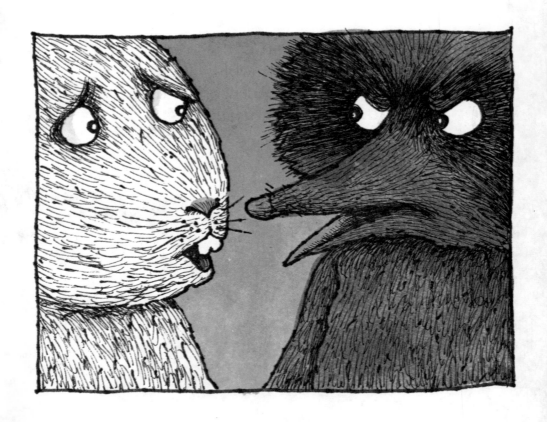

Raccoon wondered why they were standing there.
But before he could say anything, Rabbit asked,
"Are you molting, Raccoon?"
"Black hair would look bad on this new rug."

"No, no, I'm not molting," said Raccoon.
"I think BIRDS molt," he said, frowning at Owl.

The animals stood in a row along the wall
and admired Rabbit's new rug.

"The flowers look real enough to pick," said Fox.
"The sun makes them sparkle," said Owl.
"It's such a cheerful rug," said Rabbit happily.
"Perhaps we should leave," murmured Raccoon.

The animals filed out the door.
"Good-by!" called Rabbit.

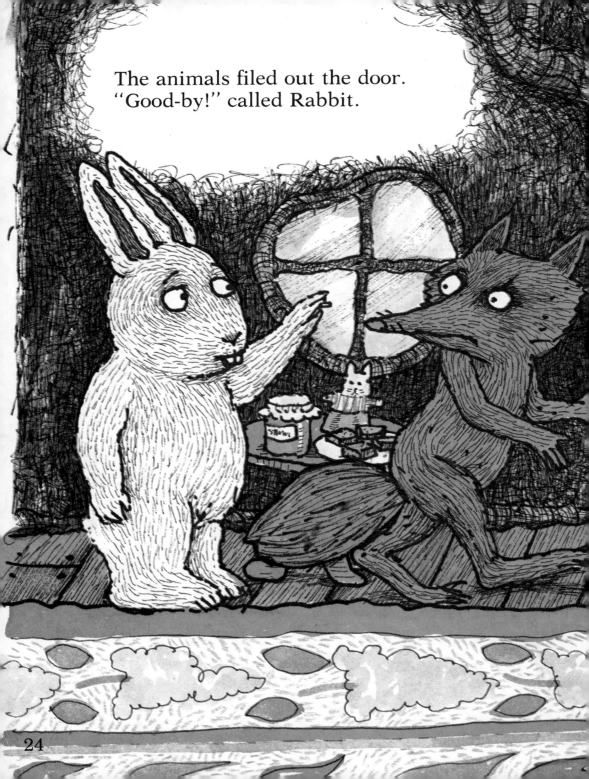

The next day Rabbit admired his rug
all day long. He felt how soft it was.
He vacuumed and brushed it three times.
He used his carpet sweeper twice.

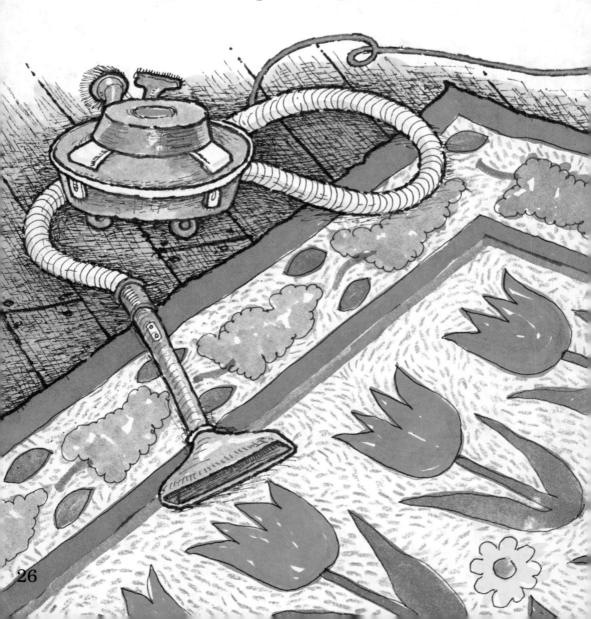

"What a handsome rug," he said to himself.
"I have never seen another like it.
No one in the woods has such a colorful one."

Every day Rabbit admired his rug.
Every day he walked around the rug
so he wouldn't make footprints on it.

And every day he was alone.
No one came to see him.
A week went by.
One morning, Rabbit said to himself,
"It sure is quiet around here.
I would bake, but I may
get flour on my rug.
I would sew, but threads and lint
would fall all over it."

29

The hours grew longer and longer.
Rabbit had read all of his books
and he was tired of watching TV.
Tears came to his eyes.
"A rug isn't much company," he said.
"I miss my friends."

The next day, Rabbit called Fox
and Owl and Raccoon on the telephone.
"I am having a party this afternoon,"
he said to each of them.

"I would like you to come."
"A party?" they each said in surprise.
"Ha, that should be fun," thought Fox.
"All of us squeezing next to the wall."

Meanwhile, Rabbit hung balloons
and streamers in his living room
and put flowers on the table.
He planned games, and bought prizes
for the winners.

At two o'clock the animals arrived
at Rabbit's house. Fox looked suspicious.
Raccoon looked doubtful. Owl looked sleepy.
Fox knocked on the door.
"Maybe the party is in the yard,"
said Raccoon, looking around.

Just then, Rabbit opened the door.
"Come in," he said happily.
"I'm so glad to see you."

"But," said Fox, "what about your new rug?"
"What about it?" said Rabbit.
"Does that mean we can walk on it?"
asked Raccoon.

Rabbit nodded.
"Well, I'll be," said Owl, rubbing his eyes.
And so they all went inside.

The friends sang, "Old MacDonald had a farm . . ."
and played Pin the Tail on the Donkey.
They laughed and talked and then
they ate pie and cake and nuts and candy.
Rabbit did not say anything when
crumbs fell on the rug.

"What a great party!" said Fox.
"What good food!" said Raccoon.
"It's a fine new-rug celebration,"
said Owl, who was wide awake now.

After everyone left,
Rabbit sat in his rocking chair.
He rocked back and forth on his new rug.
He looked at the bright flowers.
All around him he saw streamers
and balloons and leftover food.
Rabbit yawned and then he smiled.
"There's nothing like old friends
to help break in a new rug," he said.

Notes to Grown-ups

Major Themes

Here is a quick guide to the significant themes and concepts at work in *Rabbit's New Rug:*

- Friendship: Rabbit learned that he must change his new rules to keep his old friends.
- People are more important than things, as Rabbit finally realized.

Step-by-step Ideas for Reading and Talking

Here are some ideas for further give-and-take between grown-ups and children. The following topics encourage creative discussion of *Rabbit's New Rug* and invite the kind of open-ended response that is consistent with many contemporary approaches to reading, including Whole Language:

- While children rarely have problems with new rugs, they do have problems with new toys. Should Rabbit share the rug with his friends, even though it might get dirty? Should a child share a toy with friends in the same way? Discuss which is more important, an object or a friend.
- Why was Owl sleepy at the beginning of the party and wide-awake at the end? This may be your child's first encounter with a creature that sleeps during the daytime and is awake at night. Although we see deer, porcupines, skunks, and coyotes during the day, most of their activity takes place at night. Bats, of course, are nocturnal, waking up just as children are going to bed.

Games for Learning

Games and activities can stimulate young readers and listeners alike to find out more about words, numbers, and ideas. Here are more ideas for turning learning into fun:

Sharing Sessions

Silly Rabbit loved his rug so much he almost forgot that friends are more important than possessions. It takes practice to be able to allow others to share something new, especially if we are afraid they might get it dirty, or break it, or just somehow take its "newness" away. If your child occasionally has trouble sharing with a friend or sibling, this Timer Technique may help ease the stress sharing can place on friendships.

You will need a kitchen timer with a bell. Foreshadow the process with your child and a playmate by explaining that you are going to play a sharing game so that both parties get a fair turn to use the item they need to share. Tell them they are going to flip a penny to see who gets to go first, just as in any game. Then tell them you are going to set the timer for five minutes (or an appropriate time to use the item to be shared). When the bell goes off, it will be the other child's turn. You will set the timer again, and when the bell goes off the second time, the two children will have a Sharing Session for five minutes. The goal of the Sharing Session will be to see who can come up with the best ways to use the shared item together. Praise all the positive ideas they give you and help them decide which ones they want to use. Then tell them it's time for them to practice sharing the item, and set the timer again. When the timer rings a third time, you can poll Sharing Session participants to see if they want to continue sharing or go back to timed turns. Continue to time individual turns alternating with sharing times for as long as they need this, or until one loses interest and wants to play with something else.

About the Author

JUDY DELTON is a busy writer and teacher. Besides her dozen books for children, she has written many articles and essays. Before she raised her family, she taught elementary school. Now she teaches writing in colleges, and on her own. From her home in St. Paul, Minnesota, she travels around the Midwest as a favorite speaker and leader of writing workshops.

About the Artist

MARC BROWN gets many of his ideas for writing and drawing while he is traveling. He often can be found riding on trains, planes, or buses — to visit schools, see his publishers, or speak at conferences around the country.

At home in an old house near the sea, Mr. Brown develops his ideas into the words and pictures that will finally appear in his books. And all along the way, he shares his ideas with children as often as he can.

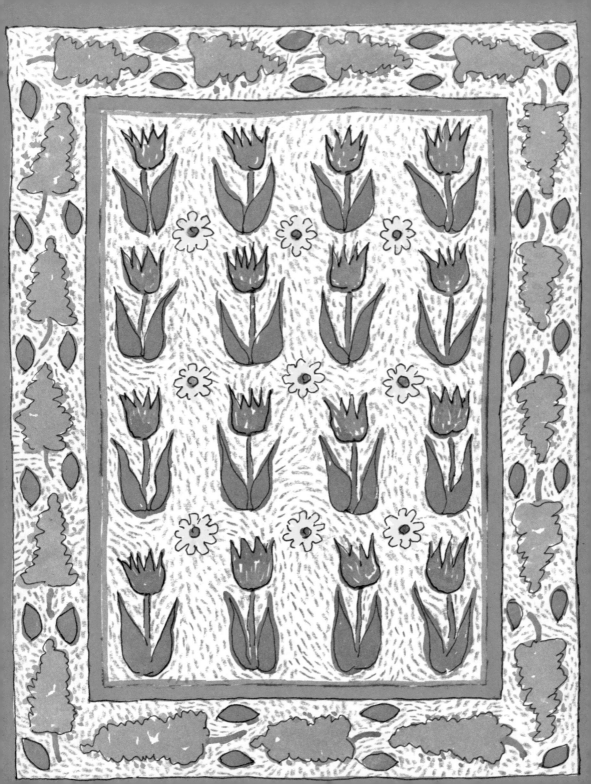

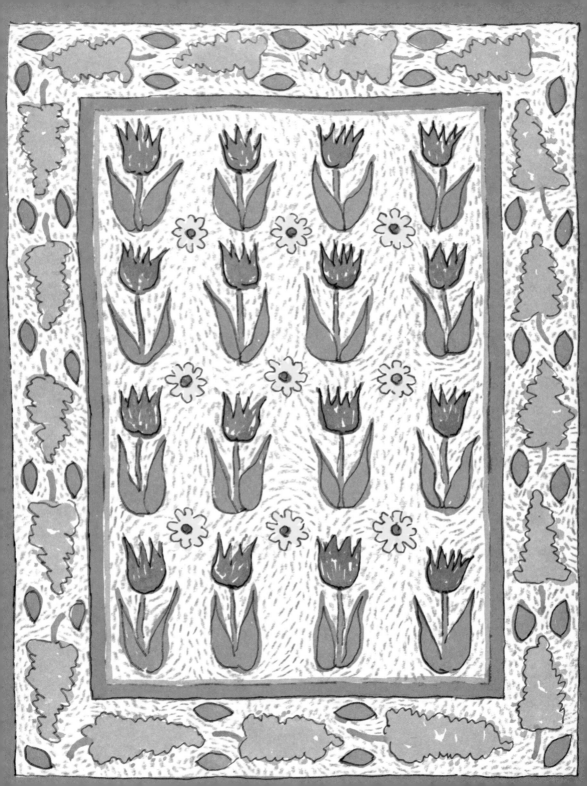